GIVING UP IS NOT AN OPTION

my journey as an international student

Anita McInnis

DISCOVERING DIVERSITY PUBLISHING
Toronto, Ontario
Canada
www.discoveringdiversitypublishing.com

Copyright © 2018 by Anita McInnis
All rights reserved. This book or any portion thereof may not be reproduced or used in any manner whatsoever without the express written permission of the publisher except for the use of brief quotations in a book review.

Printed in Canada

First Printing, 2018

ISBN   9781792101274

Dedication / Prologue

This book is dedicated to my husband, my two sons, Sean and Stephen, and my brothers and sisters, especially Beverly who had to sign all my documents including the I-20 form. It is dedicated to all international students but most notably Shanda, Sherly, and Paul who all went to Hocking College in Nelsonville, Ohio. Lastly, this book is dedicated to the many mothers who left their children and went to the United States of America (USA) to study.

More and more, I realize the miracle of God's love because He has given me a wonderful husband, a partner who believes in my dreams. Alvin, you are my joy, my confidant. Thanks for the many sacrifices you made for me. I could not have made it without you.

Introduction

My journey started with so many obstacles. My family and I saw many challenges, but through all of it I had goals and determination. The truth is, we all have our different journeys, and we all have different goals. How we face the journey, how we believe in ourselves, how we manage when things go wrong, that is what tells us who we are. Participating in international education was an essential key for me because it unlocked one of the many doors in discovering who I was/am on my journey. It taught me important aspects of life that I would not have learned had I stayed in my country. This book is going to speak to my journey and my challenges, and it will share with you the ways in which my decision to not give up changed it all for me.

Contents

Dedication / Prologue	*iii*
Introduction	*v*
The Plan	9
The Journey	15
Culture Shock	19
Budgeting	23
Control Your Anger	25
New Awakenings: College Life	27
Reality Hits	29
The Strong Determination	33
The Church Family	37
Graduation	39
The Uphill Struggle	43
Light at the End of the Tunnel	47
New Beginning	49
More School	51
The Transition	55
Look Inside of You	65
Why I Wrote This Book	73
About the Author	*ixxvii*
Mother's Pride	*ixxix*

chapter one

THE PLAN

PROVERBS 16:19 says, "A man's heart plans his way, but the Lord directs his steps. The steps of a good man are ordered by God, and He delights in his ways." My name is Anita McInnis, and I am from Montego Bay, Jamaica. I was born in Montego Bay, but I spent the first 18 years of my life in Patty Hill, Hanover. My parents' religion is Christianity, therefore I started attending church at a very young age. I am the sixth child for my mother. My parents were very poor, but they taught us the values of life. Honestly, we rarely had all that we needed, just the basic life commodities really, but we did have love among us. We were a close-knit family, and my parents made it very clear to us that we had God and each other. My mom taught us that if we had one finger of banana, we should share it and make sure everyone got a little piece. It is from these roots I write. This is my story.

Growing up in Jamaica was fun and carefree for me. We knew our limitations, so we learned how to be creative and to be content with what we had. In spite of the poverty, I was able to go to school and even graduate from college. I attended Rusea's High School, and after my graduation, I went to live in Montego Bay with my eldest sister, Beverly. In Montego Bay, I attended Montego Bay Community College. From there I worked at various places like Marguerite Restaurant,

Holiday Inn, and Airpak. I'm a people person, so I really enjoyed working at all of these places, but I always knew that I wanted more. You see, I have always been a hard-working woman on a mission — I just didn't know what that mission was. At one point, I owned a clothing store that my sister managed for me because I had so many other things on the go. I would go to places like Curaçao and the USA to purchase fabrics and clothing to sell in the store. I got to see some incredible places before we shut it down due to break-ins from thieves. What an intense time in my life. We knew that people stole, but it was still so hurtful and surprising when it came to our things! But, there was certainly a silver lining in this era of my life because it was around this time that I met Alvin. I'll spare you the love story but know that it is a good one; it's just not the point of this book. After we got married, we eventually had two wonderful boys: Sean and Stephen. You'll hear more about my family later.

After Alvin and I got married, the time came for us to decide where we wanted to settle our family. We had already been travelling back and forth to the USA, so we decided that was where we wanted to go and live for good. By this time, my Sister Delores, who is now deceased, was filing for my mom to stay in the USA, so I had hoped that my documents would come through fast enough to get us settled. I gave birth to Sean, our eldest, in Jamaica, but while we were in the USA on one of our trips, I became pregnant with my second child. I really have to tell you how this happened (well, hopefully you know *how* it happened, but I want to tell you the story). Both my husband and I come from big families, so we decided we wanted only one child... little did I know that God had a different plan. I had missed my menstrual cycle for the month but did not say anything to my hubby because I wasn't overly worried. But, one night Sean, who was eight years old at the time, knelt down at the side of his bed and said his prayer. Then he got up and went

the plan

into his bed. Oddly, he came back out, knelt down again and said, "Please, God, could you please let my mom and dad give me a little brother or sister." I was very nervous when I heard him praying like that because, well, I know how prayer works... and sure enough I found out I was pregnant. Of course, after Stephen was born and grew old enough to drive his brother crazy, whenever they had a disagreement Sean would say, "I am sorry that I prayed that prayer because I was the one who asked God for you to be born!"

Yes, you can laugh. It's all truth. God hears and answers prayer not only for adults but children too. By the time I was seven months pregnant, I decided I would go back to Jamaica because I had heard stories about children born to non-immigrants and what could happen. I got a bit scared and made the decision to go back home. My husband and I decided that he would stay in the USA and Sean and I would go back home to have the baby. Labour and delivery all went smoothly, and Stephen came into the world a happy, healthy baby boy.

After Stephen was born, I went back to school doing draperies and cake decorating. I really enjoyed it, but I wanted more. One day while reading the newspaper, I saw an advertisement about a school called 'Western Hospitality.' It was affiliated with a college by the name of 'Hocking College' in the United States. I got very excited because I felt in my spirit that this was my opportunity, so I took the number and called the school. An appointment was set up for me to go in and meet with them. The interview was great. I attended Western Hospitality for a year in preparation for college abroad. I then applied to Hocking College, and I was successful. I was overjoyed! I did not know what this degree would bring to my life; all I knew was that this was my season, and I had to do it! Before I applied though, I had a mixture of emotions. I know it's natural to feel emotional about

giving up is not an option

leaving home to study abroad, but I was so overwhelmed with excitement at the prospect of starting a new chapter in my life that I could barely contain myself.

There were nights when I could not sleep because I couldn't stop thinking about what was ahead for me. After a while, excitement wasn't my only feeling. I was filled with a mixture of joy and sadness. I was joyful because I wanted better for myself, and I strongly believed I would do well. I was sad because there were times when doubts came to my mind about whether or not I was actually going to make it there. Have you ever had this feeling? It's all mixed up - I could feel it all the time, but I really just had to make a decision in my mind. I was going to do it, nothing was going to stop me... not even my feelings.

I had a long list of things I had to do before I left which included a lot of packing, bill payments, last minute errands, making sure I got my children's report cards, immunization cards and so forth. The last few days were very stressful. One thing that helped me a lot during this time though, was talking to other people who had done the same program that I was about to do. They had been through the process, so I could relate to them. Thankfully, they offered sound advice that made me a little more calm, just a little.

Amidst the stress of planning to leave, going to study in the United States was an investment of money as well as investment of my time. But, the whole time I had the picture of what the end would be like. I saw my family healthy and happy. So, even with all of the fear and doubt, I knew it made no sense that I start something and not finish. I decided to go all the way. I realized there was no perfect moment to try something new. I came to the conclusion that I must go forward and that giving up was now not an option.

the plan

By attending Western Hospitality, it opened the door for me to obtain a student visa and attend Hocking College in Ohio. My children had visitor visas but because I did not show enough money in my account as to how they would be cared for financially in the United States, they were denied student visas. I was not going to leave them behind, so I decided to take them on their visitor visas. For those who do not know the difference between a visitor visa and a student visa, let me explain it to you. Visitor visas are non-immigrant visas for persons who want to enter the United States temporarily (six months) for business, tourism, pleasure or a combination of both. You have to prove that you have no reason to stay. A student visa is the first paper that proves that you have gained acceptance to a known educational institute in any foreign country. You have to apply and be accepted by a student and exchange visitor program, and you have to show financial evidence that you can afford to be there for the duration of your stay. After your final exams, you get a work permit for one year. After a year, if you want to renew in status, you have to go back to school. Being out of status in the United States is a violation of immigration laws and may cause you to be ineligible for a visa in the future. I was not going to get myself stuck in any of that mess, though. I decided to make as much money as possible in order to make sure that my family would be ok.

So, in preparation for the move, I sold my car. Actually, I sold everything I could get my hands on because I really needed to have some money to at least pay for my first three semesters. I was going to reside in America! I used to say to myself "O Lord, let me sell everything so that I can have money for at least one year." Remember, international students were not given student loans, so we had to know how we would manage financially... So... My house was rented, car sold and any gadget or item of clothing possible was sold. Eventually, I was totally ready to go to this "land of opportunity" not knowing what awaited me.

God has a plan for each of us. His crowning work of creation came on the sixth day when God created human beings (Gen 1:26), "Let us make man in our own image." As God looked around Him, He pronounced His creation to be good, that included you and me. The Psalmist David says in Psalms 139:15-16, "My frame was not hidden from you when I was made in the secret place." When my dad's sperm and my mom's eggs came together, God already knew that I would be a part of creation. When I was woven in the depth of the earth, God's eyes saw my unformed body. You and I have a purpose here. We just have to be courageous enough to stick it out. From the beginning, God knew each of us, and He has a plan for us. He also said in Jeremiah 29:11, "I know the plans I have for you, thoughts of peace and not of evil to give you an expected end." Because I can reaffirm who I am in Christ, my behavior begins to reflect my true identity and His plan for my life. God looked at Adam, and He saw a world changer. He looked at Abraham and saw a nation builder. He saw David as a king. What did He see in me, Anita? He saw potential! He saw a mighty woman of valor, a cake decorator, a counselor, a great chef etc., and so he said, "my daughter, for you - giving up is not an option. The journey may be tedious, but it is necessary for you to become who I created you to be, and therefore the journey must continue."

chapter two

THE JOURNEY

IN December 2000, I migrated to the USA with my children and another student, who was my friend and was also going to the same college. We spent Christmas in New York with my hubby who was already living there. It was a great Christmas. The 1st week in January, my friend, my youngest son and I boarded a greyhound bus for Columbus, Ohio, which was more than a 14 hour ride. My eldest son was left in New York with his dad. I need you to just imagine the night before we left. Yes, it was very emotional. I hardly slept. I spent most of the night crying. I felt guilty about separating my family and fearful of the unknown. I could hardly make eye contact with my husband. Even though he was not stopping me from going, just looking at him, I could see a lot more than what he was actually saying. I saw pain, fear, loneliness. It was all there. And knowing the responsibility he was going to bear, especially financially, was heart wrenching. At that moment, I felt like it was the best time to change my mind. However, I dried my tears and reminded myself of my reason for coming to America and pushed through the feelings of wanting to quit. I was going to go to college and improve the lives of everyone in my family.

Living arrangements were made for us by the college. It was a predominantly white town, with many students from all over the world; I was in awe of it all. I mean, now

I'm in college in the USA! It was all so mesmerizing.

The day that we arrived in Nelsonville, we had to start registration and orientation right away. I was running around that whole campus with a three-year-old on my hip. His presence was definitely the most challenging aspect. When I tried to get him into a nursery it was too expensive. There was no way I could afford any form of daycare, so I took him with me to class the first day. Everything was happening so fast, and it was all so exciting. And then, the excitement of our new space smacked me right in the face. The professor told me that my son could not stay in the class. I was near to tears. I felt the professor was so unreasonable. I did not think twice taking my son to class. I truly thought that he was so young that it would not be a problem, and at the very least, I thought that the professor would understand why I had my child with me. But it was not so. I panicked, then I got very nervous and angry. I said to myself, "Oh God, what if they say I cannot continue school? What would I do?" As all these thoughts were going through my mind, my friend said to me, "Do not worry" as we stepped out the class with my son. My friend's friend was the President of the International Student Body. She called her and told her the situation. The president had just finished her class so she said she would keep my son for me.

That was just the beginning of my uphill battle of college with my three-year-old. Thank God for good classmates who helped me by babysitting Stephen while I was in class. Being at home and studying was a different story.

Accommodations were made through the college for us to stay on campus or at a private house. I chose the private house. Stephen and I shared 1 bedroom in a 4-bedroom house. Every morning I had to get him ready, get myself ready and rush to get the bus. Some days I would have no idea who was going to be watching him while I was in class. There were times I would be in class and could not focus because I was thinking about my son and the choice I made to keep him with me. I continuously went back and forth in my mind; was it the right decision? I was also worried about the fact that he spent all of his time with different adults and had no other children around to play with. The good thing was that he was a very quiet child so everyone enjoyed keeping him which, of course, made life much easier than if he had been a restless child. I am very grateful to have had, for the most part, helpful, caring friends who helped me in taking care of Stephen.

Not everyone around me was supportive, though. One time, my friend made a comment that he had never seen a three-year-old in college. Even though he found it to be funny, and I believe he did not mean any harm, I still felt a bit of guilt and as if everyone pitied me... which made me feel uncomfortable many times. I felt like everyone was saying, "Here comes that poor woman in college with her poor child." Those could have just been my own thoughts though. I could not shake the feeling of guilt about my child being deprived of having friends of his own age. He also did not get quality time from me. Reading bedtime stories to him was very limited, and there was not much time to play with him or take him to McDonald's, or even to watch a show together. I would put the TV on for him to watch, and I would study. I was always worried about what people must have been saying about me as to why I had to bring him with me. To be honest, I shed so many tears that year that it's difficult to look back on. I remember asking myself frequently, "why don't I just quit and go back to New York? What am I so passionate about?" The answer that always came back was, *Giving up is not an option*! The truth is that beyond all the tears and fears, somewhere deep down, I knew that I was headed for greatness.

On Thursdays we had Accounting; it finished at 9pm. Let me stop here to say we had one school bus, and it stopped running at 5pm each day. We had to walk home or carpool with the few who were able to purchase vehicles after any class that ended after that time. Every Thursday night after our class, I had to depend on someone to give me a ride and then pick up my son who would be in different places (depending on who could watch him). Most of the time if and when we had to walk home, we would take a short cut which was approximately 2 to 3 miles, and which included a walk on the train tracks in often 20-degree (or less) weather.

This went on for a while; it was so hard for me. Most nights I would cry, but I had to be strong for my son and for myself knowing that success is the progressive revelation and realization of God's plan for my life. As Jeremiah 29:11 says, "For I know the thoughts that I think toward you said the Lord, thoughts of peace, and not of evil, to give you an expected end." I knew that I had to stay strong.

In spite of the entire struggle, I was able to maintain a GPA between 3.6 - 4.0; I was on the Dean's List and the President's List. I had to make the most of every moment that I was away from my son. I studied on the bus, in between classes, and whenever I could. I did not wait for the last minute to study because I knew if I did, I would not be able to be successful. Having my son with me at college was challenging yes, and school itself was challenging, but what I learned about myself was invaluable. I learned that I can do anything with God by my side and that through determination and hard work I can make my dreams come true.

chapter three

CULTURE SHOCK

WHAT is culture shock? Culture shock is an experience a person may have when he/she moves to a cultural environment which is different from his/her own. I came from Jamaica and went to the United States. The temperature, the fast pace, the subway, and the educational system was almost too much for me. The intense feeling of homesickness was very evident for me. American customs at restaurants, in the classroom and in everyday life often felt strange because I wasn't used to the culture, so I knew that I had to do something about it.

Getting involved in student groups was one way of eliminating some of the loneliness; likewise, getting involved also helped me with my school work. In any case, I knew that I had to make wise choices in every matter to stay ahead of the game (otherwise, I knew it would take me under). For instance, I always befriended students who were very smart. I partnered with most of them especially when I had projects to do. I would take the time at least once a week to talk about the content. I would sit with them in class. I was aware that my influences needed to bring me closer to my vision, not further; this thought pattern was pretty normal for an International Student. We typically had our brains *on* all the time because we knew what the sacrifice was to be there.

I didn't stop there though; I actively sought out people who had already taken the class. Students would tell me what the professor was like and what I could expect, so I would go into a class knowing the professor's tendencies and how he/she operates; it was much easier for me. Lots of professors recycled tests, so if those people kept their old ones, it was also good for me. I did not consider it cheating at all. It was just logical. I never lost focus on the fact that it was my academic passion that brought me to the United States in the first place. I had to focus on my studies.

As soon as the semester started, I would make sure I signed up to get a counselor to help me with any challenging subjects. I was a bit intimidated to ask questions in class because the teachers were different than back home. In Jamaica, students had a different level of respect, and I wanted to make sure that I was being as respectful as I would be if I were home. At the end of class I would talk with the professor if I was unclear on an assignment. They were open to help me and that meant a lot, and made me feel like I was going to make it in this strange and wonderful land.

I found having a study group was an excellent way of studying but also a great way to feel more comfortable. Not only did I learn the material better, I had a great support system to laugh with, cry with and make it through the perils of college with. If I needed extra help, I got it. If I needed an ear to listen to me, I got it! We international students stuck with each other to make it through the cultural shock that we were experiencing.

In Jamaica, as I mentioned we grew up quite poor however, we always seemed to have what we needed. But here in America, dealing with money and health was something I was not used to. College in the United States is expensive. There was no financial aid and even health insurance was a risk. We could end up with big medical bills in addition to our education, and room and board costs if we weren't careful.

Let me talk to you about medical bills (still a bit of a sore spot for me!) One time I had a dental issue and couldn't afford to go to the dentist. My friend felt so bad for me and decided to help me out. Well, she gave me her insurance card, and I went to the dentist. Guess what? When they called my friend's name I was sitting down and did not respond. They called about three times before I realized *I am my friend!...* I was a nervous wreck because I was impersonating someone else and also because it was out of my character to do such a thing. My tooth problem was solved, but I would never do that again (I doubt it could even happen today, with all of our advanced technology). In the end I didn't even have to pay this bill, and it still bothers me! You can laugh all you want or say what you want to say as you read this, but don't say you would never do that. Like I said, there is no financial aid for international students; you have to make sure you have enough money to take you through. If you are lucky enough, you may be able to get a part-time job on campus - jobs which may include positions in the school cafeteria, library, bookstore, or gym. A part-time job helps with your books or personal expenses. For me though, even if I could get a part-time job I had my son with me, so I wasn't able to work without daycare.

Fortunately, I had a good support group. It consisted of the Coordinator for International Students, the President and my friends from Jamaica and around the world. The President of the International Student Body was a very understanding person. She was so supportive and helpful; I don't know what I would have done without her. The large group of students that came from Jamaica and other countries provided me with emotional and physical support during my stay. I got to know many students in my program.

No matter how you look at it, international students coming to the United States can face a lot of challenges be they cultural differences, social challenges or financial issues. The food is different. The clothing is different. The religion is different especially if you are not grounded in your own beliefs, it can be a big challenge. You have to know exactly what your beliefs are, and know that just because you're in college you don't have to be swayed by just any kind of doctrine. Culture shock led me to feelings of frustration, anxiety and homesickness, but I was able to experience only minimal amounts of these, as I created a solid network that helped me through.

When we arrived, most of us, as international students, did not have winter clothing. One day, one of my friends was so cold that instead of gloves (which he did not have) he wore a pair of socks on his hands. Luckily and shortly after that, an International Student Counsel person took us to a church where there was a great amount of clothing, bed linen and other winter stuff we could have for free. Their support was life changing because without them, we would have had a really tough time in that cold weather!

Another funny incident was when my friend, who is a Seventh Day Adventist, was attending a function at her church. Prior to that day, they had told everyone to bring a "dish" which means *bring something that you can share with others*. They were having a potluck... My friend took a large bowl with her to the function. When she arrived at the door, they asked her if the dish that she brought was hot or cold. My poor friend was so shocked because she had taken a big, empty, deep bowl with her! She said nothing and then hurriedly went to her seat and hid the empty plate under the chair. That was a laugh!

chapter four

BUDGETING

IN our new environment, everything seemed to be going wrong and felt very complicated. Even when the frustration slowed, and we knew how to face some of the challenges that we encountered, there were still more things. I had a tight budget and remember, I had my son with me; I had to make sure that we were both eating from the money my husband sent me.

A friend of mine was in a better situation and, on many occasions, she would bring dinner for us or take us out which was a wonderful luxury. Sometimes when we were on school break I would go to New York, but the 16-hour Greyhound bus journey and the cost of the tickets were so much, that at times it was just better to stay; but the thought of going home to New York and getting some real home-cooked food and my own Caribbean food pushed me to go. I remember once I went to New York and of course everyone had a list of what they wanted me to bring back, from an aunt or cousin, who would drop off something for them, be it the Bronx, Brooklyn or Long Island. It was much cheaper than mailing it... *You should have seen me with the large boxes going back on the Greyhound bus.* Thank God I did not have to pay for extra luggage! One particular time when I came back, I brought back some curry, and my friend said he would cook some curry chicken. We put the money together and bought a few pounds of chicken (one person could not afford to buy it for everyone). Word of mouth spread, and soon everyone wanted some curry chicken. My friend cooked and cooked and cooked, and guess what? After sharing out all the food, my poor friend did not get any. That was not funny, but it sure does illustrate how life was as an international student.

Another depiction of life as an international student is seen in this story: One morning my roommate missed the bus. She did not want to be late for school, so she decided to rent a bicycle. The only problem was that she did not know how to ride the bicycle. She was determined to learn however, because she knew she had to be on time for school. She struggled with it for awhile, and then made the decision to walk. She, like me, knew giving up for her was not an option. Many people passed by and saw her, but no one even thought of helping her. Eventually she saw a classmate coming along on his bike, and she figured he would help her out, but the young man said to her, "I'm very sorry; I cannot help you! I am late for my class," so he rode on his way. Nevertheless, giving up for her was not an option. Then, all of a sudden, she saw another young man who started to laugh and ask her why she is not riding the bicycle, he said, "It can't be that hard! I wish I could help you, but I am late for my class, also." He hurried along leaving her alone to struggle with her new project - the bicycle. Luckily the bus had to drop off something back at the college, so my friend was able to put the bicycle on the bus and catch a ride. You see, determination has to do with the final goal not the ways in which we get there, after all.

chapter five

CONTROL YOUR ANGER

TWO weeks after that we were having an Award dinner for all the international students, (my friend just recently reminded me about this. She said I gave her a beautiful brown blouse to wear to the ceremony.) She always liked to take pictures. We took a lot of photos, but one classmate took a particular picture of her and decided she was not going to give my friend the photo she had taken. I am not sure why. An argument developed, and my friend went to the police on campus to help her get back her photo. She said some silly things in her anger, and long story short, my friend almost got locked up because of her hot head.

    The lessons I learned from the incident are that in everything we have to think before we speak. Anger will not fix anything; it will only make it worse. "A wise man thinks first, and then speaks, a foolish man speaks first, and then thinks." In the heat of the moment it is easy to say something you will later regret. My friend did not focus on how she could resolve the situation; her only focus was what the other student did. In life we have to remember that yes, we will get angry, but we must be careful how we express our frustration. You can express your frustration in an assertive but non-confrontational way. The Bible speaks about anger in many ways, like in Ecclesiastes 7:9 it says, "Be not quick in your spirit to become angry, for anger resides in the heart of fools." Also Ephesians 4:26, "Be angry and sin not. Let not the sun go down on your wrath." This story was an example of college life lessons. I learned so many things while I was there.

chapter six

NEW AWAKENINGS: COLLEGE LIFE

ANOTHER illustration of how life was as a college student occurred in the house that we shared, which was a 4-bedroom with 2-bathroom home. I was the oldest person living there and so most of them called me "Miss Mac." Again, based on our culture, we were taught to say "Miss so and so" or "Mr. so and so", not like today where everyone is called by their first name. On this particular night, my son was asleep, and my friend and I were studying. I had to go to the bathroom, but while I was there I heard this banging. I thought someone was at the door, but after listening more closely, I realized the banging was coming from the other room. There was a little peep-hole that I was able to see through, and sure enough what I peeped had me in disbelief. There was a guy and a young lady making out (having sex), and it was not the guy's girlfriend... My mouth dropped open and my mind was racing off like lightning. I turned in surprise and called my friend, "Come quick, let me show you something." I took her to the peep hole and all I heard her say was, "Help, Jesus." I pulled her away and then I looked again. We got ourselves together and went back to studying. How much studying we did that night I cannot even remember, because our minds were so taken up with what we saw. I didn't know this was part of college life. The next day when I saw the young lady in class, I could not even look at her. The thought of what I saw the night before came right back. Now, this wasn't culture shock. This was an eye-opening, wake up call. I was now a college student. My naiveté was beginning to lessen. The world was beginning to look a little different. Nonetheless, I continued to meet new people because meeting with students with different values and beliefs helped to widen my cultural awareness, gave me new perspectives and improved my social skills. I came across many people I probably would not have met at all if I had not gone to college in the USA. I also learned of the culture and policies of other countries. I wasn't just getting an academic education, I was also getting a social/cultural education!

I faced many challenges as an international student, but no matter what it was very important to hang in there with other international students, because we understood the things that we went through; things that no one else really understood.

chapter seven
REALITY HITS

AFTER the first semester, I couldn't manage to keep my son with me anymore. I had to make the decision that either I was going to quit college or take Stephen back to New York to stay with his father. Really, I was ready to give up, but I had come so far! I reminded myself that giving up was not an option for me. But, I was still torn apart. I felt terrible because my husband already had his hands full with a 10-year-old and working to help me in college, (he had a very long commute) and now he would have to take on a 3-year-old! After much discussion, he said I should bring Stephen home. So here I was bringing Stephen to New York; a 14-hour ride on the Greyhound bus, only wishing I could afford the plane ride.

With help from my extended family, Alvin was able to keep both boys, but not without struggle. As for me, there was no excitement bringing him back to New York, only guilt. Guilty because I was now leaving both of them with my husband. What if they resent me because of my absence? What if they become sick and I am not there to take them to the doctor? What was my husband thinking but not saying out loud? It was overwhelming for me. Oh God, decision making is not easy, nor should it be because it has the power to change the outcome of one's life forever.

giving up is not an option

The decision between pursuing my goals and raising my children became a burden I felt I could not handle. I knew I was a good parent and a great wife, but I had dreams and goals that spanned beyond my family. Even though it hurt so much, I was the one who made the decision and I was not going to give up. I decided that studying would not stop me from loving my children. I did not want to use them as a reason to turn down an opportunity to make something out of my life. With regards to my husband, I knew that the financial pressure, long working hours and taking care of two young children would be very difficult and could damage our relationship. I kept repeating that concept in my mind. However, there was this inner feeling pushing me, *Anita, you've got to go to the finish line*, and so I pressed on. I realized that no situation is permanent and nothing lasts forever. The reality is that we always have choices regarding the decisions we make, our thought process, what we feel and what we will do about a situation. We have to learn to keep things in the right perspective. For me it was keeping my vision in front of me and working hard. Life is no bed of roses, and there will always be ups and downs, especially towards victory. My downs were good for me because they helped me to appreciate my ups.

Personal Chapter for My Husband

Alvin, there is no greater reward than one that is reached through personal dedication and hard work. You have proven it to be more than so. Over all these years, you stood by the family. Thanks for being such a wonderful husband and father. I remember you told me to choose something that I really enjoyed and you would help me in whatever way you could. You have made so many sacrifices, and I know in my heart that God made you especially for me. Our strengths and weaknesses are being woven together to create a beautiful life. We think so differently, see issues from different perspectives, respond differently to the things that happen around us. But look, wow look — I'm getting really emotional — with God's grace and mercy, we have learned that our differences are the very qualities that give our marriage strength and color and vibrancy. As we work together, we will continue to work ourselves into a great masterpiece. Of course, we are two different people with unique personalities. But, guess what? You will always be my hero. Our marriage has not been the perfect fairy tale, but you will always be my Prince. You have stretched me in all kind of areas, the way nothing else ever could. As I live and learn in our relationship, I honestly believe I become more loving and compassionate. Sorry for the times when I took some things for granted. If I were to make a two columned list of your traits, with the positives on one side and the negatives on the other side, the good would far outweigh the bad. In fact, your positives are so overwhelming. I really appreciate you. I am sooooooooo glad you are mine and I am yours. I believe you are the best. I still remember the first time when you held me and asked me "Can I kiss you?" You are such a gentleman. I also remember the first Oxford dictionary you bought me. All the things that you have done are so amazing especially the sacrifices you've made. When the boys were in private school and I was in college, you deprived yourself of so many things. Now you can spend time on you. I just want to highlight a couple examples of the phenomenal person you are...

You kept a journal about the boys, and I want to share something that you wrote. "Guys, the true meaning of success is not how many people you have passed on your way up, but how many people you have helped. Because the amount of 'many' might not count but touching people's hearts will always be remembered, so try not to be the kids of cash and coins but kids of hearts. Guys, I have a big secret to tell you, A DADDY'S LOVE IS NOT JUST NOW AND THEN, DADDY'S LOVE IS FOREVER."

I remember every year before we received our American documents, you would send me and the boys on a church retreat, and you would stay and work. How many men would do that? Once Sean, our older son, rented a cable movie without us knowing. When the bill came, you told him you will take it from his allowance, and you would not give him any more allowance for a while. Unknown to us, you saved all the allowance, and one day you said, "Sean, I need to speak to you." Sean was nervous, and he whispered to me, "Mom, what did I do?" You handed him an envelope and in it was more than $300.00. Of course, there was a good lecture from you. I do not know how much Sean remembered, but for sure he was more than elated to get so much money. You would be, too, wouldn't you?

Yes, my readers this is a little about my hubby. He really did push through the trials and now we celebrate our triumphs. We will continue to trust God and push on. I will endeavour to become all that I can be in our marriage. I will be kinder, more loving, more patient. I know it will take time, commitment, and most of all God to make my love for him complete. I will always love you, honey.

chapter nine

THE STRONG DETERMINATION

AFTER Stephen left, I studied harder. I remember the days when we had finals. A group of us would study together until the wee hours of the morning. We would study and then two or three of us at a time would take a nap, while the others continued to study. My friend would make breakfast and then off to school we would go. Back then, as international students, we did not believe in getting B's; we had to get A's! We worked very hard. At the end of each semester, when the college had a special dinner for achievements, 90% of the students were international. We had goals. We refused to be limited by resources or racial barriers. We let nothing stop us.

One time I asked a classmate (who was not an international student) if he had passed the class. He said, "Oh, yes! I did! I got a "D". I was like, "Really? What?" He said a "D"! I almost passed out. I reflected, looking at the fact that I had a three-year-old child in college with me for much of my studies, and I did not have the resources we needed to eat and live well, yet here was someone who had a golden spoon in his mouth and felt good about getting a "D". That was ridiculous to me. But, I suppose everyone has their own journey and challenges and, as I mentioned, my success did not come without its own difficulties.

giving up is not an option

I remember when I had to take Microsoft Access, which was a very challenging course. Microsoft Access is a database management system. It was finals, and I had to pass the subject in order to graduate. I wrote a note to my professor and this is what I said, "Professor, I cannot do this exam. I am leaving, Anita." On the same piece of paper, the professor replied, "Anita, I know you have the potential and the ability. You can do it. Remember you need the subject in order to graduate." After I got the response from her, I went to the bathroom and I started to cry. My professor believed in me and there I was in self-pity. Honestly, although throughout the book I keep saying, giving up is not an option, that day was so tough that it really had me wondering if I could really make it. Maybe it was the thought of leaving my family for such struggle? Maybe it was just the course? I don't know, but in any case this was rock bottom for me. Thanks be to God, at that specific time someone was there for me. I often think about what would have happened had the professor not cared enough to push me? You may be asking yourself *isn't she telling us that giving up was not an option for her, so why now? Why this challenge?* Well, let me tell you. At that point, my mind was taking over. I was seeing myself as a victim and not a winner. The truth is whatever occupies your mind will direct your actions. All I could see at that specific time was; *you have tried your best and this is where it ends for you.* I was struggling to see any further than that. Let me tell you this, you can do all the physical changes you want to do; you could change your diet, the car you drive, you can change your job etc., but if you do not change your thoughts, there will not be much difference from what you have been getting. You cannot do it by yourself though, you must have God's divine intervention. Thank God in advance for the outcome. You'll be surprised at how He carries you. I forced myself to thank God - it took everything that I was.

That day, my friends came to the bathroom, and they

hugged me and said, "Anita, we know you can do it! We refuse to leave you in the bathroom. We will all be graduating together."

All of a sudden, I remembered all the sacrifices I had made to be there: leaving my family in New York, leaving my country, starting something totally new. It was difficult, but I had made it through not having enough money to purchase all of my course books or even enough food to eat! I dried my tears and thanked my friends. I told them to leave and that I would be in the class soon. One of them, by the name of Shanda who was like a daughter to me, stayed with me until I got myself together.

I eventually went back into the classroom. Thankfully, the professor gave me some extra time, and I finished the exam! How did I do it? I prayed in my heart for God to assist me. By this time, most of the other students were finished and only a few were left behind. My fingers were trembling as I touched the keyboard and my mind was thinking all kind of things. I prayed to God to help me to remember the things that I learned. While it was all flooding back to me, I remembered this verse in the Bible which says, "The memory of the just is blessed." (Proverbs 10:7) God helped me, and at the end of the semester, I got a "B", and I was on the Dean's List. The next time I saw the professor, she said, "Anita, I am so proud of you. You did it!" I said to her, "Thank you for believing in me even when I gave up on myself." I know it was divine intervention that day because I passed with a "B" when I thought I would fail. I knew I wanted to make it, but I needed extra support, and I got it - from God and His angels (my teacher and my friends). Microsoft Accounting was challenging for me but, fortunately, I had some great things that helped pull me through some dark times.

giving up is not an option

chapter ten

THE CHURCH FAMILY

LIFE in Nelsonville was interesting. Amidst some barriers were some great spaces. One of the spaces that brought me great joy was First Baptist Church Of Nelsonville Ohio led by Pastor Chunn. Pastor Chunn was and still is the pastor of this small church, but he and the members have *big* hearts. They took all of the international students and fed us both physically and spiritually. They were very kind and compassionate, and not only in the spiritual realm but they were very, very practical. Sorry to say but in our churches today, things like this are lacking. We are very great at feeding the spiritual man but not the physical. There has to be balance and this is what this church did. They were so kind and compassionate which today are two qualities that seem to be in short supply. There was nothing that they would not do for us. I will be forever grateful for them.

On Sundays, Pastor Chunn or the deacon would pick us up for church. Every Sunday after church they would have dinner prepared for all of us. Even at our graduation, all of us were given an envelope with money in it. These people were just exceptional. A couple years after graduation, I was invited by Pastor Chunn to speak at their International Student Day which was a blessing. I felt honored to be chosen to represent the international students, because being an international student has changed the way that I

giving up is not an option

live my life in that I do not walk around in self-pity. I take responsibility, and I don't blame anyone else for my circumstances; and that is mostly because of all that I experienced (both good and bad) while being an international student.

Now I purposely eradicate fears of failure. "God has not given me a spirit of fear but of a sound mind." I am full of potential. I am headed for greatness. Every so often I look at myself in the mirror and say, "You go, girl! You are headed for greatness." I know I will not let the odds come against me. I will not tell myself "I can't". I also know that how I think and my attitude will determine how long I am going to remain in any given situation.

There are many great lessons we all learn from life. I learned a great deal of mine from becoming an international student in America. I have learned to believe in myself, and I have realized that I am capable of doing anything!

chapter eleven
GRADUATION

GRADUATION was something I knew I had to do for myself and for my family. It was a huge accomplishment for me. At Hocking College, students could invite as many people to the ceremony as they wish because the graduation did not require a ticket, but for many of us, we only had the support of each other. There were no parents or husbands in attendance. My hubby could not attend because he was the only one working, and to take the day off plus the long journey would be too much. I knew I had his support and his prayers so that was enough for me.

The ceremony was fantastic. One of the things that amazed me was the dress code of the graduates. They wore anything under the gown. For me, in my country, you are very well dressed for such an occasion. Wearing that cap and gown was a great accomplishment for me which brought tears to my eyes (still does, actually). I could say I did it and knew it was something to be proud of. College is not for everyone, but it was for me. I had to finish! It was such a moment of victory as I walked across the stage to receive my degree.

After graduation, many of my colleagues went to different places like Florida, Ohio, New York, and there were those who went back to Jamaica. Some of my friends had graduation trips planned for the summer, while others including myself, needed to start working immediately. Now that I could go to work, I just wanted to "Go" although, in hindsight, it would have been nice to take some time to reflect on my life and decide what is best for me; I did not. I did however, walk away with the memories of the things I had learned, the experiences that I had in college, and the amazing people that I met while there. I really did grow to love the college that brought me and my friends together. I cannot even imagine having gone to another college, not that it would matter. What does matter is that I have learned that graduating from college stirred up all kinds of emotions within me. It is huge and real, and it is definitely something I am so proud of because it was such an incredible feat to push past fear and doubt and decide not to quit but to become victorious.

After graduation, I went back to New York and applied for Optional Practical Training (OPT). This is a permitted 12-month working period for undergraduates and graduate students on F-1 visas who have finished their degrees or who have studied in the United States for more than nine months. During this time graduates are allowed to actually work and be paid (this is heavily restricted while one is studying, though.)

I got my first job at Sunrise Executive Hotel where I worked as an inventory store person. I worked there for one year, then I had to register in school again to get another work permit. This time I worked at the Marriott Marquis Hotel as a housekeeper for another year because, (even though I had the qualifications - an Associate degree in Hotel and Restaurant Management) I had no experience. I wanted a job badly because I knew my intentions of becoming financially independent. The only job available at the time was housekeeping. Three managers interviewed me and each

graduation

made the same comment "Anita, I see here you have an Associate degree, why housekeeping?" My response was that *there were not any other openings*. I just wanted to get my foot in and then I would transfer to another department. They were sold, and I was employed. I worked for one year and then went back to college (Monroe College) to acquire my Bachelor degree in Business Management.

I did extremely well at Monroe College; I was even on the President's List. After achieving my bachelor's degree, I was employed at Mt. Sinai Hospital as a Financial Specialist. I worked very hard, but the job became too stressful, and I resigned. I got another job at a publishing company, which was only part-time.

giving up is not an option

chapter twelve

THE UPHILL STRUGGLE

I once went for an interview at a hotel in Manhattan, and it went very well. I knew the Sales Manager personally, but her boss said even though I had wide experience in the hotel industry, my resume showed that I only spent a year or less on a job. I did not want to explain to them that, as an international student, that is what happens; one cannot work anywhere for longer than 1 year. I did not get the job. It felt like there were so many odds and limitations against me, but I knew I had to beat them, and, well, you already know my mantra; *giving up was not an option*.

My uphill struggle continued as I did many odd jobs… and I mean many. Yes, I had a bachelor's degree, and yes, I was doing housekeeping jobs and babysitting. I could not get any jobs even though I had a degree because I did not have any experience in my field. I was not prideful though, so I was willing to do anything for survival. Also, my husband had spent so much money on helping me get through school for so many years that I did not want to just sit and wait for a specific job. I was willing to do anything. Plus, I had to have money in order to go back to school every year anyway.

In 2008, my whole world changed. I lost my sister, my landing papers were not arriving for my citizenship, and my eldest child was going off to college! It was almost too much

giving up is not an option

to bear. The even tougher part about it was that all of these pieces happened one at a time. Sean finished high school and did very well so college was the obvious next step for him. My first born going to *college?!* But here's the thing, he did not have a social security number to register! What do I do? Well, to start, I cried and cried. Sean really wanted to go to NYIT College. It was his dream. Honestly, it seemed impossible and I felt awful, but remembering how much of a struggle I had as an international student, I decided that our faith would be what was best to pull us through this time. God was going to have to take the wheel. One day, I said, "Sean, you better go online and register." He said, "Mom, how am I going to do that when they ask for my social security, and I don't have one?" I told him to try and try and try; something will work out. He did, and I strongly believe that it was by a great miracle that he was successful. I can't explain what happened, but for some reason, the school accepted him. We even got a call to tell us that he had been granted a half scholarship! We were elated! And so, my son, my eldest child, was able to start college. That is what you call divine intervention. You see, when your back is against the wall and everything seems hopeless, that is when God steps in. He is the God of the impossible. I want you to pause for a moment as you are reading this book----are you pausing? Take some time to think about what miracles God is performing and has performed in your life. Grab a journal; write them down. They are important to remember when you are feeling down and like your back is against the wall.

    As an international student I could travel, but it was very limited. Work permits lasted just for a year. I was just waiting for my Green Card. Years had passed, and as I mentioned, I worked several jobs. All of my brothers and sisters were fine. They did not have any issues like I did. But, when I was finally ready to become a landed citizen and was awaiting my papers, my sister became ill and passed. It was

the uphill struggle

very hard and challenging for me. I had to stop, look up, look down and sideways, wondering where was God in my situation? Had He forgotten me? Where do I go? From whom do I seek help? It was only God's mercy that kept us. But, boy, it was tough.

What is one thing in your life right now that seems impossible and has consumed you day and night? Of course, while it was happening to me I put on the mask and appeared as if it was ok, but I was so broken; nothing seemed to be happening for me (other than Sean getting into school!) As you continue to read, may I remind you that God is a covenant keeping God. I may have had my degrees, but my immigration status was looking impossible. I wondered when I would be free in this country of great opportunity. It hurt to the core when I saw others who have "golden opportunities" in this country not doing anything productive with their lives. Then I asked the question, "Why don't I have what they have?" (which was the great Green Card.) Those who are citizens or those who are green card holders have opportunities that I could only imagine, and it cut me deep knowing that I was being stopped, and even my children at times were being prevented from living their dreams. For those of you who don't know, a Green Card refers to an immigration process of becoming a permanent resident. It is proof that its holder is a lawful resident, and it allows them to work without having to stop every year like I had to. I knew that having it would open up my floodgates to prosperity.

People from all over the world are willing to sacrifice almost everything to come to this country. There are so many mothers who have left their children back home for six or even ten years just to attain the American dream. Their children do not even remember who they are. They have become strangers to them. I wonder how many family members have died and they could not go home to show respect because if they go, they cannot come back to America. Listen to me, no matter if you've got a Green Card or you have always been a citizen, you've got to respect the determination and sacrifice that people make to live in this beautiful country. I was in this place, and I continued to wait and hope in the midst of adversity. I had to be patient. My advice to you is to remember that it is not over until God says so. Your joy is coming. Giving up was not an option for me, and surely, it is not for you either.

Your dream may be getting through school, but studying is so hard. Please do not give up. Your goal may be finding a good job but all you face is rejection. Please do not give up! Your desire may be to repair a broken relationship, but you encounter hostility and disdain. Please do not give up (if the relationship is right for you). Maybe it may be a bad habit you need to replace. Maybe your burden is your wayward child. Please do not give up on them. Be it your Green Card, a new home, or an exercise program, please do not give up. Keep your dreams and goals before you. Continue to work hard. Look in the mirror every morning and speak to yourself. Eliminate all the negative people from your life. I had to do all of this, especially during my toughest times.

chapter thriteen

LIGHT AT THE END OF THE TUNNEL

THE tough times persisted until one day, one fine Tuesday afternoon, my phone rang and it was my lawyer calling to tell me about my paperwork and my interview appointment. My freedom was almost here. Wait, I almost forgot to tell you this part... When I realized that it was time for college for Sean, and I did not see any way out of our predicament, my husband and I discussed divorced because if we did and became single, it would be easier for me to get my immigration status. I got a number for a divorce lawyer, and I told him my story. He agreed that for the benefit of our children, it would be easier if Alvin and I divorced. He asked me on what grounds I would be divorcing. I did not have a clue! Alvin and I had a great relationship; we just needed our children to be able to go to college. He told me to speak to his secretary, and make an appointment to come see him the next day. That next day never came though, because when I got off the phone I went on my face, and I started bawling (crying) to God. I reminded Him of His promises to me. Like when Hezekiah in the Bible got the news to set his house in order because he was going to die, and what did he do? He reminded God of his faithfulness to Him. A friend of mine was at my house while this was all happening. She knew me as a very private person, so when she heard me crying, she probably assumed it was terrible news from back home. But then she undoubtedly realized what was going on when

giving up is not an option

she heard me yell, "God, I will not get divorced! You have to come through for me! I will have my Green Card!"... And... well, you already know that I got it, I just needed to tell you that story because I want you to understand that life is filled with challenges. Keep your principles intact and trust God to come through.

Two weeks after that, I got my date for my interview, but guess what? My first son and I would be able to do our papers in the United States, but my hubby and younger son had to go back home! "God, are you really serious?" This was a half joy- two out of our family of 4 had immigration papers to be done here and the next 2 had to go to Jamaica. "Oh no! God, I will not settle for this!" That was another set of weeping. I could cry now just thinking about that moment!

Remember at the beginning of this chapter I said that three things were happening in my life simultaneously? My sister became ill, Sean was trying to go to college, and I was waiting for my Green Card. My sister becoming ill while I awaited my Green Card was the hardest part because I really thought I was just going to give in and give up. I'm saying this now having no idea what that would have looked like. There is no quitting when you are losing someone - there is simply nothing to do. So, I just waited. Losing her was so painful. Thank God though, I was able to make it to North Carolina to pay my respects.

chapter fourteen

NEW BEGINNING

AFTER my sister's funeral, I got a job at the Dime Saving Bank as a Teller. I worked there for four years. I applied two times for a managerial position with no luck. After some time, I felt that I couldn't grow there. I knew that I needed to try something else. I had a part-time job in the health field at the same time, so I really wasn't too worried about leaving. There are times in life when we must move on. Having a back up plan is necessary, but it is crucial to grow. If you are somewhere that is stunting you, weigh out the options; what else can you do? You'll need to remember that when you are not growing, you're dying. Choose to grow and move on.

The part-time job in the health field was a very good one, and the money was great. So when the family of the person I was taking care of wanted someone full-time and offered me the job, I was elated. They were offering way more than the bank was even paying, so I took the job. It was a full time gig but after about 3 years the patient died, and I was jobless, again.

What was I going to do? What do you think I did? I am an entrepreneur. I had some money put aside and so I decided to open a clothing/bedding/draperies store in my basement! I also made juices like Irish moss, green juices, and I made cornmeal puddings, bread puddings, and wedding cakes. I could sell anything. I bought low, and I sold high. I transferred the skills that I used in Jamaica and made myself some money in America! It wasn't a full time gig, but it did bring in some money and kept me busy; I felt like I had some purpose. I knew that it wouldn't last forever, but it was good for the time.

I wanted to maintain my independence because even up to today, I do not know what it means to pay half of the bills or rent. My husband always took that responsibility. It was just my personal bills that I had to pay (you know how we ladies love to shop... I cut back a lot now...)

Let me just stop to say a big thanks to all of you who have been always supportive in all that I do. A very special thanks goes to Alvin for always, always supporting me. I am so grateful for you. Another special thanks goes to one of my many friends for whom I will be forever grateful. She has and is always there for me. There is nothing too hard for her to do for me especially when it comes to finances. I have to give thanks also for the many ways that God has blessed me. Life as an international student was hard, yes, and it was even harder becoming a US citizen, but I happened to have been blessed with people in my life who really wanted to see me succeed. Countless times, the two of them helped put me through so much education that I have lost track.

chapter fifteen
MORE SCHOOL

I had done a CNA course (which stands for Certified Nursing Assistant), the phlebotomy (taking of blood) course, and so many others. I knew so much about so many things, but unfortunately the knowledge was not helping me make more money.

One day, my sister said to me that I should really start taking courses that were relevant and could actually get me a job. She suggested nursing. She said even though I have a bachelor in business, it would be better if I went into the professional health field. I told her that everyone was not called to be a nurse… and then I took most of the prerequisite for the nursing program anyway. I stopped after realizing that nursing was not for me, but I kept going with the Certified Nursing Assistant (CNA). You're not going to like or enjoy everything that you try. I don't think you are supposed to. But, you do need to try things. You need to step outside of your comfort zone and discover more of who you are - at least that's what I did.

The first time I went to work in a nursing home it was only 1pm and I was not finished with the patients. I went outside and called my sister to ask her if I could go home. She said, "You better go back inside and be professional!" I went back in to complete my shift, but I certainly never went back after that. I tried it... it wasn't for me!

This type of partial work went on like this for a while and then came the drought. I mean a drought. It literally felt as if God had turned His back on me. I was still running my store, but it wasn't enough. I needed more, but there were no jobs for me. Almost every morning I would get up and cry. I sent out resumes until I felt sick. One day, my sister said to me, "Anita, I wonder if anyone has done something to you, that not even a cleaning job you can get." (This is in reference to Obeah or dark magic like a curse, but I do not run my life with such thoughts!) I told her never to say things like that. Even though it was a drought in my life and I felt abandoned, I knew God had a plan for me. But, the real struggle for me at that time was keeping myself motivated. When nothing pays off, it becomes really hard to find the energy and the mindset to begin any kind of activity. The financial aspect of this situation was killing me. Look, my husband had done his best and now I needed to be assisting him! I was the one who had the degree, and I had no job?

My unemployment was taking a heavy toll on my family's financial stability, and even though my hubby was not criticizing or attacking me, I felt terrible like I was more than a burden to him. You see, going to college was different, by now I should have been working and assisting with household bills, but it was not so.

There was also the psychological toll this jobless situation was taking on me. The situation was messing with my head! Not having money with little to no prospects of making money had me in a serious slump. Apart from losing almost all my confidence and motivation, I reached a point where I felt that I was gradually losing my ability to think straight. I was so obsessed with finding a way to earn money that I became aggressive, yet nervous. Many times I

more school

even became angry because I saw people doing fine or better than I. I felt jealous. Through my green eyes, others seemed to not to have a care in the world, and I was struggling day in and day out. There were days when I would wake up and feel like I despised the whole world and other days filled with pure sadness. It was like finding myself at crossroads, but every road was closed. I felt, at times, that the real possibility for me was permanent unemployment and that was very scary. I did not go to college to study and make all those sacrifices for nothing! I still had (and have) dreams I want to realize. I just needed a job and with that came the happiness of going to work and being able to assist my husband. But all of that seemed so luxurious and far away.

Myles Munroe said, "It's not what happens to you that matters, it is how you respond to those events." God wants all of us to prepare for change. Change will happen with or without you and I. Whether we approve or disapprove. This time in my life was one of my defining periods. I really had to ask myself if I knew myself... like really knew myself. Did I really know my self-worth, my self-image? What about my self-esteem? Did I still believe that I could be anything I wanted to be? What was my purpose on earth? Why was I now facing these limitations AGAIN? Then, God reminded me that I was created in His image. After a lot of deep thought and internal work (which included prayer, crying and more prayer and more crying), I realized that I needed to make a change.

giving up is not an option

chapter sixteen

THE TRANSITION

OUR lives are in a constant state of transition, and transition isn't always fun, but you still have to carry on. I attended Bethlehem Missionary Church for over ten years where I was grounded in the word. I also attended Bible School there and was the bursar. I was taught how to pray back the word to God. For example, my Pastor would say things like, "according to Your word God, he that winneth souls is wise; therefore, based on Your word, I want to be wise, so I am going to win souls for the kingdom." I learned so much there, but I needed to learn more. My life had to change.

In 2010, I started to attend Faithful and True International Ministry. God did transfer my life totally for His glory. I taught at Bible School often, and my Pastor once sent me to officiate a funeral service. That was an experience for me. I learned so much about God's power and what He has given me, but still, I was without a steady job! I had my documents---I was a citizen of the United States of America. I thought I had everything in order and that everything would be smooth sailing. It was not so for me. Do not get me wrong, and may I pause to say God blessed me with my husband who provided me all of my basic needs. He could not have done more. How he did it all, only God knows, but he kept the family together. I will be forever grateful to him. But, I wanted more! I kept asking myself, "Anita, can God trust

giving up is not an option

you? Can He really trust you with the test you are currently facing?" At times, I would say, "sure He can," but there were other times when I failed the test miserably, and He could most definitely not trust me. There were specific lessons He wanted me to learn. He reminded me that my present situation was the path that would lead to the conclusion of the test. So eventually, I developed the motto, "Get up and try, again!" I can accept the thing called failure, but I cannot accept that I will not try again because I am never alone. God is with me. Sure I have been short changed sometimes, but giving up is not an option! So I had to press my way forward. I think that one of the biggest lessons I have learned from this time in my life is that it is not the failure that matters but what you do with it that does.

Beyond the emotional turmoil this period of time put me through, it was also upsetting having to deal with others during that time. The worst part was having to talk to them. People would say, "How is the job hunting going?" Or, "Keep your spirits up, something will come soon." And, "You will find a job before you know it, the economy is terrible but soon it will pick up." Sometimes I just wanted to scream at them even though I know they meant well. One time, someone said to me, "One day you will look back on this as a positive experience no matter what you do or learn during this time, and when that happens, you will have to tell someone because only when you have been through some serious challenges can you tell someone." I now understand.

Desperation determines destiny and giving up will not bring about what we want. As Myles Munroe, a great man of God once said, "Just as there is a forest in every seed, so I am certain there is a new world within your world. Men and women who make changes in history are those who have come against the odds and told the odds it is impossible for the odds to stop them. Do not throw yourself away.

Do not let anyone else throw you away-- because you are up against some odds."

You may not understand my story because you were never an international student, but I am sure you can empathize with my plight. Perhaps things were never like this for you; regardless, you have a story. What are some odds you are facing as you read this? Do you remember that there were many times you felt like giving up? Did you give up, or did you hang in there? No matter your answer, I want to remind you that whatever God calls for, He provides for. Do not lose your identity. There are so many people watching to see how you are handling the circumstances in your life. But, no matter what, you do not have to fight your battle alone. Take your position, stand firm, and watch God work in your life. Do not be afraid; do not be discouraged. Go and face your giants, and the Lord will be with you because He is your source. You may not identify with my story but what about the times when you think you don't know yourself? What about the times when you feel like you are falling all the way apart, and it seems like nothing can put you back together. Well, here's the thing - knowing yourself is very important. You must know your self-image, self-esteem, and self-worth in order to manifest your destiny. You must be self-aware because knowing yourself will help you to improve on all that you do. Remember the time you thought about giving up, but look at you, now! You're closer to your dream than ever before.

Even as you read my story, reflect on your journey and be thankful that you did not give up. If you are someone that gave up, I have news for you; there is still hope, and there is still spiritual strength. As a believer with personal

giving up is not an option

experiences and a personal relationship with God, I know that prayer has a power that can change the worst situation into a beautiful world. God loves us all, and He can and will heal the broken-hearted. Reflect on the exciting plans you had for your life. Where are they today? What happened? You may have a lot of excuses. You may have let go of your dreams because you did not get practical or responsible. You may have given up on the the possibility that you could have the life you desire. But, it is time to ask yourself, why? What got in your way. Whatever it was, it is not too late. Please do not say that you are too old now, or not experienced enough or talented enough. Whatever is limiting you or allowing you to give up, think again. Ask yourself why God may have created you. Decide what is your purpose on planet earth! I beg you to realize that there is someone out there in a very similar situation who pushed through these negative circumstances to *MAKE THEIR DREAMS A REALITY*. Don't let life get you down. It is never too late or too soon to start taking steps towards what you desire. Dreams are what allow us to live a full and meaningful life. Yes, I am still talking to you, you who quit, you who say you cannot — I am talking to you! Yes, the dreams that you had can still be a reality and that passion that you had which set your heart on fire must continue to burn. That thing that has always excited you, allow it to awaken you, again! Do not settle for a life of defeat. Do not let anything keep you from claiming what you are meant to pursue. If you can dream it, you can do it. I hung in there, you can, too. The Bible teaches that man is a three part being: The Spirit, Soul and Body. We learn to survive with our personality but ultimately our temperament and character reveal who we really are.

  In 2016, I got a part-time job at New York Presbyterian Hospital, and also with the Department of Education as a Substitute Teacher. Currently, I am doing my Master's in Christian Counseling with National Christian Counselors

Association (NCCA) as a Licensed Pastoral Counselor. The name of my Counseling Ministry will be 'Created to Conquer.'

Is it possible for you to be anything you want to be? Yes, you can because you were created in the image of God, not superior but *exceptional*! Our God created temperament which is the identity given us at birth. It is that part of us that determines how we react to people, places and things. If we could only know who we really are and our purpose here on planet earth it would blow our minds. Sometimes we want to be who we were never created to be. God did not design you and I to wear masks, but we are so good at doing it. Be it the mask of religion, mask of shame, mask of who you are not; when you can be honest with yourself, take the mask off, look in the mirror and see *You*, and say to yourself "You are fearfully and wonderfully made", then and only then will you appreciate and celebrate *YOU!* Stop the pretense, especially older adults and mothers in the church. Too often we pretend as if we have not gone through stuff. If only we could let the younger generation know, that understand too because we have been there. We need to let this generation know that we too have been there and can support them through.

You see, because after all of these years I am also a licensed marriage officer, a Reverend, and a baker (specializing in wedding cakes). I do the counseling, I bake the cakes, and I perform the weddings... Do you see the hand of God in my life? Can you see the journey?

And when the journey is done? I have been asked before how I want to be remembered and now I know. It will not be because of money because I do not have any, but I want it to be about the legacy I leave behind. I want to be remembered for the number of lives I have impacted. Here's a sweet story:

giving up is not an option

I remember a couple who had some immigration issues. The husband was American, but the wife was undocumented. It took her a long time to get her papers. I felt her pain. She was at the point of giving up. Even though I was not working during this time, I borrowed $2000.00 to lend them, so they could submit the documents. You may think this decision foolish because I was not working. I mean, what if they did not give it back? Where would I get it back to repay the loan? I certainly did put my integrity on the line, but I trusted God and remembered the passion I have for international students and those trying to make a new life for themselves in a new land. Well, let me tell you, today she is a part of the American dream. She has her documents, and when I heard her say that I played a vital role in her still being in America, I wept and gave God the glory. I am grateful to have impacted her life.

There was another young lady who was not an international student, but she tugged on my heart strings, and I knew that I had to join her journey. She smokes, and she is often high on drugs. I remember one day I saw her, and I took her home to let her take a shower. I gave her clothing and just let her be herself - I did not need her to change. I only needed her to feel well and great even if it was for one day. God is good all the time because today, she is off drugs and is in nursing school!

What is your story? We are all on a journey, and we have all reached a place in our lives when we felt like giving up, when we felt no one has ever gone through what we are going through, not even Job in the bible. As you read, you may even be in the midst of your pity party, but I dare you to dry your tears, finish reading, and tell yourself you will not give up, you will arise and become who God created you to be. Myles Munroe said, "The wealthiest place in the world is not the gold mines of South America or the oil fields of Iraq or Iran. They are just down the road, the cemeteries. There lay buried companies that never started, inventions that were never made, bestselling books that were never written, and masterpieces that were never painted. In the cemetery is buried the greatest treasure of untapped potential."

May I say that as human beings, after our basic needs are met, we always endeavor to pursue fulfillment of our higher needs for safety and security, love and affection and self esteem. Few individuals reach the state of self-actualization, in which one functions at the highest possible level and derives the highest possible satisfaction from life. But, it must be a goal for everyone. In order to self-actualize, you have to:

1. Accept yourself (as humans we are imperfect despite the fact we are wonderful)

2. Respect yourself (recognize your abilities and talents and take pride in them)

3. Trust yourself (learn to listen to the voice within you)

4. Love yourself (be happy to spend time by yourself)

5. Look at challenges as opportunities for personal growth (learn from your mistakes)

6. Think of not only where, but also who you want to be a decade from now (the goals you set, the decisions you make, and the values you adopt now will determine how you feel about yourself and your life in the future.)

I have experienced all of these. One of the most useful ways to self-actualize and achieve my goals has been my habit of positive thinking and talking. I narrow down the type of people with whom I keep company. I refuse to be in the company of negative people. People who have no sense of direction and who do not believe in my dreams can occupy no space in my life. I love myself, and I am proud of my accomplishments. I believe in myself, and I know I am headed for greatness. There is a song that I learned in Sunday school when I was a girl that seems perfect for this moment. It went like this, "I am a promise. I am a possibility. I am a Promise with a capital P. I am a great big bundle of Potentiality, and I am a promise to be everything God want me to be." Success is not just about getting to where God wants you to go, it is about who you become in the process. As we come to the conclusion of this book, I want you to ask yourself these questions.

Who created me?

Who do I ultimately trust?

To whom do I look for ultimate truth?

Who do I look to for security and happiness?

Who is in charge of my future?

Then, I want you to think about a goal you have wanted to achieve. Think of the thing that has given you such a strong desire that you *know* you have to accomplish it. It is there and will not go away, right? Why? Well, it won't go away because God created you to do it. You need to finish what you started. Go forward and achieve! Do not give up halfway. Discover where you are right now and take action. Remember the story of the Prodigal son in the Bible? That God-like moment that changes everything. There was no one else around. It was just him and the pigs, but he had that awakening. Then, he experienced the brutal honesty where he came to himself and then took action.

Have you ever learned something about yourself or

had someone tell you something and it completely changed things for you? You were awakened to some truth and from then on you could never unlearn or unhear it. Well, if this is something you have experienced, it is now time to take action. Whatever your purpose, you can beat the odds. That dream you have, please let it become a reality. Giving up was not an option for me, and it must not be for you. Finish what you set out to do. Finish as the Apostle Paul did, "I have fought the good fight. I have finished the race, and I remained faithful." (2 Timothy 4:7) Also think about this line from Psalm 5:12, "The favor of God translated into good ideas. The Lord will bless the righteous with favor. Wilt thou compass him as a shield?" Do not; I repeat, do not let your dreams die. You can do it! Beat the odds and tell yourself, "Giving up is not an option" and trust me, you will be headed for victory!

giving up is not an option

chapter seventeen

LOOK INSIDE OF YOU

THERE is a miracle inside you. You may have a broken heart over some issues in your life, but you are breathing right now as you read this and that is a miracle in and of itself. It is who you choose to become in the process that will decide your fate. Your purpose will come from your pain, and your pain is your purpose. Therefore, you've got to press on. God wants our brokenness not our perfectness, because none of us are perfect. Many a person has failed in life because he or she gave up too soon. Look at this illustration from a story in the Bible about a man named Caleb. He waited for 45 years for a promised reward. He did not look at the circumstances or listen to the people around him. If he did, he would have lost his faith and given up hope, but he trusted God and refused to give up (Joshua 14:6-15). Forty Five years was a very long time to wait for a promised reward. May I ask how long have you been waiting for a change in your circumstances? That child that you want so badly, how long have you been waiting? Don't you quit. Some folks at Caleb's age would have given up long before and made a graceful exit in a rocking chair, but not Caleb. He still trusted God. He still stood on God's word and had faith in God's promise. Finally, his opportunity came to claim the promise when Joshua subdued the Canaanites and peace came. His generation was all dead, except he and Joshua who had survived the "wilderness wanderings" and death on the battlefields of Canaan. He could now claim the inheritance as one who had lived through it all.

Look at this saying by Caleb who was 85 years old, "Give me this mountain!" Are you kidding me? Your question might be why are you telling me about this man? That was in his day, today is different. Guess what? Jesus has not changed. Yesterday, today and forever God remains the same. Caleb asked for the hardest place of all, a place where giants were and where the fierce Anakim guarded the cities. Sometimes, we do not understand why disappointments come our way, often times they come at no fault of our own, but new opportunities will come our way if we hold steady in our faith, continue to trust God and DO NOT GIVE UP.

Take a look in the mirror; put the book down for a little while. Look at yourself. Who are you? What do you see? Look again, don't you see God's creation? I want you to look until you see someone who is fearfully and wonderfully made. What others may think about you is not important. What does God think about you? It is time to believe in you. You are an asset and not a liability. What others think about you is their opinion, but what you think about yourself is your reality. I have made a lot of mistakes, and I am sure you have too, but I am better than all the mistakes I have made. Do you have what it takes to continue the journey no matter what? Yes, I know you do. I now can forget the mistakes of the past and press on to greater achievements for the future. There are many projects that I have started that require my continued persistence. I know, with God's help, I have what it takes to continue my journey no matter what. That is my integrity.

My reputation and integrity are very important to me. Remember to treat people well. You need to take time to think about whether others can count on you. Can you keep your word? In spite of your story, make sure your reputation stands out. Let it be your personal brand. When you are off the scene, how will you be remembered? Whose life will you impact? It will not be the Master's degree or the PH.D, or the money you have in the bank, but the ways that you treated others and the powerful changes you made. Make sure that you have a great legacy to leave behind. My desire is that after I am off the scene, people will remember who Anita really was. I want to be remembered as a woman of integrity, a woman who stood up for righteousness, a woman who decided to beat the odds. I want to be remembered as a caring woman who always tried to be there for her friends and family as much as possible, a woman who was never afraid to check up on her friends just to know they are okay - calling different states and Caribbean countries just to say hello. A woman who tried everything, be it baking, cooking, counselling etc. I want to inspire people, I want people to be reminded that if I went through all of that, then they can press on and become who they were created to be. No matter what the obstacle, have faith that something good will come out of it. In everything, I've learned to be dependent on God, to trust Him even when I felt like giving up.

My journey makes me who I am today. My journey is towards living a life of purpose. I have, and will continue to impact lives. My extended family and some of my friends meet almost every Sunday evening. I cook, and we sit and fellowship. For me, Thanksgiving is every Sunday at my house. I just love to cook and enjoy "Today" to its fullest. I believe so much in practical living. In 2014, I started a Bottle Drive Ministry. With it, I say, "Do you have a Passion for Souls? Why don't you join me in my Bottle Drive Ministry? I collect bottles, sell them and give the proceeds to ministry, so when we are going on missionary trips we can buy what we need. Recently, I also started to help widows in India. From my bottle drive every month, I send money for

giving up is not an option

these women. I am so proud of where God is taking me. I also host Mother's Day functions and Valentine's Dinners. There is no way I can erase any part of who I am. I have learned to listen more and speak less. Come with me and let us push forward and make your journey a success. Do not stop dreaming. But most of all, do not put limits on yourself. Age has nothing to do with it. God said He will *beautify the meek with salvation.* You will have to TAKE CONTROL OF YOURSELF AND MOVE FORWARD! Moving forward is the first step towards starting on this journey of life, and in this journey of life, you have to make choices. When you need a job and you pray until your knees are sore; if you do not get up after praying, get your resume together and send it off with more prayer and fasting that God will grant you favor, nothing will happen. You have to take action. You have to empower and motivate yourself on this journey.

I know I am a woman on a journey. I am valuable. I am of purpose. I stand on the promises of God. God said He will uphold me with His righteous, right hand. You know what? I am excited to tell you that I am being held by God. Every journey is different and while mine continues, I have found out that by understanding who I am I am better equipped to assist others.

Today, I have learned many lessons that money could never have bought. I have become stronger and wiser. For instance, before I started being a counselor, I received confirmation from Isaiah 50:4 that stated, "God has given me the tongue of the learned to speak a word in season. He opened my ears to hear as the learned He opened my eyes." Truth be told, I was scared. I mean, I had already been through so much just trying to get there that I didn't know what to think. I was worried about how many people would think that I wasn't good enough, and I wondered if I should even try… But I pulled through. I decided to put those thoughts aside. What about you? Are you afraid of tomorrow and the "what ifs"? Are you afraid of being criticized by others? People will give up on you when you fail, but you dare not give up on yourself! Losers are those who never try anything. Do your best to look at challenges as opportunities for personal growth. Learn from your mistakes and move on. Think positive and speak positive. Life is full of challenges, but remember you and I can achieve any goal we want to achieve once we have the potential, believe in ourselves and most of all, let our total dependency be upon God.

Today, I am proud of myself. I believe I can climb any mountain because of the love and support I have shown myself, but mostly because of the love and support from my wonderful family. They are my joy. There was a time that I had to go to the hospital. I was only there for two days, but my younger son, Stephen, didn't want to come and see me while I was there. I questioned it, but I didn't really think too much of it. Weeks later, when I was out of the hospital and back to normal, I came home from work one day, and Stephen asked to go to the park with me. I had just come home, so I was a bit tired, but something within me knew that I needed to go. When we got there, I could tell that Stephen wanted to tell me something because he was talking about the weather and other odd things for a young person to talk about. To be honest, I was concerned. My heart was pounding so fast. I wanted to make sure that I was open to him and what he had to share. When he finally opened up, here is what he had to say, "Mom, I love you so much. I NEVER want anything bad to happen to you. I couldn't come see you in the hospital because I was scared, and I didn't want to see you sick in the hospital bed." He told me about all the things he was scared of and about his journey. We cried together and sat in the park for a little while before we went home. To me, that was one of the sweetest moments of my life.

giving up is not an option

Recently he gave me a birthday card. A part of it reads (in his own handwriting) "I do not love you because you cook for me, or clean, or you are a Christian or because you have a degree. I love you because you played a part in my creation. I get to experience the phenomenon called life because of you. Because of you, I get to experience love, happiness and joy. My generosity, my happiness, my loud carefree laughs come from you. Your love for me is unconditional, Mom, and I will always love you." My heart fluttered for hours after I read this. Something like this money cannot buy, and I am very proud to know I have made a great impact on my children's lives. I am proud to know that who I am has affected people in a positive way.

Your outcome is shaped by you and God. Being a person who has made up her mind that giving up is not an option, I know that I, Anita, have a destiny that is determined by God Almighty. Where I come from does not matter. It should not matter for you, either. Even if you were made in the back seat of a car or in the bushes, you are not a mistake. You were created in the image of God, and you are created for a purpose. What matters is how God determines the outcome, and He will surely will. God is the one who writes the script of all of lives.

I challenge you to continue the fight, keep focused, trust God to see you through and remember no matter what, "Giving up is not an option." The greatest obstacle known to finishing what you start is ultimately, You! We have so many fears, anxieties and doubts. But, the truth is, if I can do it, you certainly can. GIVING UP IS NOT AN OPTION.

Arise and become who you were created to be. Please, as I come to the end of my book, my desire is that whatever God's plan and purpose is for your life that you will fulfil it before your time comes and you are no longer on earth. In the process though, make sure God is the center of all your plans. In every aspect, do not leave Him out. Be careful of 'Dream Killers,' for they will set you off course. Use your God given brain and your mind. You will need help along the way but be very discreet. Acquire the information you may need, as not everyone will be happy for you. Everyone will always have an opinion to give you. I believe such opinions are usually the cheapest things.

giving up is not an option

chapter eighteen
WHY I WROTE THIS BOOK

I wrote this book because I wanted to remind my readers of who they were created to be. Stop telling yourself lies that you are old, stupid, incapable. Identify the lies and arguments you tell yourself as the truth. "I am above and not beneath, and I can do all things through Christ that strengthens me." Think about the three trimesters a pregnant woman must go through. She cannot give up halfway; she has to push to the end. Like the pregnant woman, you must tell yourself, "I do not look like what I have been through." The pain you are feeling is not because of what you lost, but because of what you are about to gain. You are on a journey and guess what? It is *your* journey. Be ready to produce and go through your labour pains. Your water just broke; it is time to push. It is time for you to step up. Whatever your dreams are, they can become a reality.

On December 2, 2016, I celebrated my 55th birthday. I went to the store, and I saw this card which I purchased. It reads, "If you can dream it, you can do it. Make your dream big. Huge. A world changer! I cannot wait to see what you are going to do - knowing you (I added my name to it). It will be great! Congrats." I use that card and read it almost every day to stay motivated. Let your dependency be upon God, and you will accomplish what your heart desires. God did not put you here to fail. Success is written all over you, and

giving up is not an option

it is very important to God that you succeed.

Before I go, I have to say a big thanks to my niece, Mica who lives in Canada. She wrote her first book, and she came to New York to do a book signing. When I told her that I wrote my book in 2001, she said, "What? Aunty, I dare you to get your information together and finish your book. I know someone I can recommend." I started, got in touch with the editor and sent in my first draft. When it came back, there were lots of corrections to be made, things I had to change. Guess what I felt... you guessed it... terrible. The whole technology thing has always been one of my greatest fears. It is one of my weaknesses, and I have to admit it. I tell you, fear is and can be one of the greatest inhibitors that keep too many people from fulfilling their destiny. Thank God I rose above that feeling and finished my book!

I want to thank my son, Sean, who helped with the technology part. So many times the editor was on the phone telling me do this or that on the computer, and I was so lost. Luckily, Sean would assist me. Thanks, Son. Sheena, my editor, thanks for your patience with me. You are a great person.

Life is short. Live today as if it is your last day and smile. The Bible says, "Laughter is good medicine." Enjoy the labor of your hand. Too often people work so hard, especially we as Caribbean people and don't enjoy themselves. There is nothing wrong with working hard, but we need to have balance in our lives. Do not wait for the time of retirement, by then there may be nothing left to enjoy. Sickness may take over; anything could happen. My advice to you today is, do what you can do. Your endurance will develop, your strength of character will increase and your character will strengthen your confidence.

God bless you and thanks for taking the time to read my book.

About the Author

Rev. Anita McInnis is a licensed Pastoral Counselor, National Christian Counselors Association (NCCA). She is also a licensed Marriage Officer. She has a bachelor's degree in Business Management. She has been married for 29 years to the love of her life, Alvin McInnis, and is the proud mother of two boys, Sean and Stephen. Her intention is that each person will be reminded that life has a process and each of us are unique in our own way.

Mother's Pride

I want to share my son's poetry with you. His name is Stephen McInnis. Stephen, I am so proud of you.

BLANK PAGES

This was a page that I skipped,

Didn't put any ink on,

no thought or feeling into, and paid no attention

This page remind me of my life

A time period where I must go back inside myself and pay attention to things I didn't before

A time to use a page I've skipped pass, and kept ignoring

Acknowledge blank pages

Stagnant relationships and suppressed feelings

Fear and confusion

Those blank pages are still apart of your book that you cannot change

There will always be uncomfortable part of the story

Always parts that you want to skip over but you can't

You will never understand your story, or meaning behind the words, characters and setting if you ignore those blank pages

My blank pages have anger, sadness, doubt, worry, loneliness,and confusion written in the clearest ink in the world

Visible to no one

But I know they are there

I study my blank pages Change is written these blank pages, but I skipped over that too.

Sometimes I don't want change.

WE Changed

They Changed

Changed.

My blank pages

I embrace these blank pages because they make me better.

They are apart of me

Overcoming the fear of these blank pages is what I need to do.

I am not scared.

I write my story of greatness in these blank pages.

My story of strength.

Nothing will be suppressed on these blank pages.

I am these blank pages.

ME.

Stephen McInnis, I am these blank pages

Made in the USA
Columbia, SC
06 December 2023